This book belongs to:

....

AUTUMN
PUBLISHING

Published in 2021
First published in the UK by Autumn Publishing
An imprint of Igloo Books Ltd
Cottage Farm, NN6 0BJ, UK
Owned by Bonnier Books
Sveavägen 56, Stockholm, Sweden
www.igloobooks.com

1021 001
2 4 6 8 10 9 7 5 3 1
ISBN 978-1-80108-105-4

Printed and manufactured in China

Disney
ENCANTO

BOOK OF THE Film

🦉 AUTUMN
PUBLISHING

Years ago, when Alma and Pedro Madrigal became parents, Pedro promised they
would leave their troubled world behind and build a better life for their family.
Alma bundled up their triplets and, by the light of a single candle, the young
couple left in search of a new home.

A group of others, who were also looking for a safe place to live, joined them on their journey.

But as they reached a rushing river, the danger they were trying to escape caught up to them. Pedro gave Alma and the babies one last kiss and turned back to fend it off.

When Pedro did not return, Alma fell to her knees.
Heartbroken, she held her babies close and prayed for a miracle.
Suddenly, her candle bloomed with magic!

Bright light blasted away the darkness and swarms of butterflies appeared, fluttering around its glow. Mountains rose, stretching towards the sky!

Pedro's promise was kept as their new home emerged inside a safe place full of wonder, an Encanto.

A house, lovingly called Casita, grew around Alma and her babies, surrounding them in protective love and magic.

Over the years, the candle burned brightly and the magic grew in unexpected ways.

The Madrigal children and grandchildren were blessed with special gifts. When the time was right, each child received a glowing door and discovered their own unique bit of magic.

It was important to Alma, who was now an abuela, that they earn the miracle and fulfil Pedro's promise. Each family member proudly shared their gift with the villagers.

Soon, it was Mirabel's turn to receive her gift. She was Abuela's youngest granddaughter.

Abuela's eyes twinkled as she looked at Mirabel. "You are a wonder," she said. "Whatever gift awaits, will be just as special as you."

Ten years later, the Madrigals were preparing for another Gift Day. The first since Mirabel's. That night, her youngest cousin, Antonio, would walk up to his door and receive his own unique gift.

All the family were helping prepare their home for the ceremony, including Mirabel's two older sisters, who were putting their gifts to good use.

Luisa used her super strength, and Isabela made the flowers bloom. Mirabel meanwhile... well, Mirabel helped the best she could.

That's because, on Mirabel's Gift Day, her door disappeared and she never received a gift. She was the only ordinary member of an extraordinary family.

Julieta and Agustín, Mirabel's parents, reassured her and told her not to overdo it and that she had nothing to prove to anyone.

Mirabel decided that, whatever her own problems were, she wouldn't let them ruin Antonio's big day. So, she went to give him a present. Antonio told Mirabel that he wished she had a door of her own, but Mirabel told him not to worry about her.

"Seeing you get your special gift and your door," said Mirabel, "that's gonna make me way more happy than anything."

Then, Antonio opened Mirabel's present to him. It was a cuddly jaguar.

Evening came, and it was soon time for Antonio to walk up the steps towards his door. Nervous, Antonio reached out to Mirabel. She hesitated, knowing all too well that her grandmother didn't want her to interfere.

"I need you," said Antonio, motioning for Mirabel to take his hand once more. Wanting to be there for her cousin, Mirabel finally took his hand.

As they walked up the stairs, the memory of Mirabel's Gift Day came flooding back to her. That day, the door that should have changed her life forever vanished, and her family's high expectations of her had altered dramatically, too.

Despite the painful memories, Mirabel continued walking with Antonio. Each step felt like forever to her, but they finally reached her cousin's door.

Nervously, Antonio placed his hand on the doorknob. Moments later, Mirabel's young cousin was filled with magic and dozens of animals flocked towards him.

Antonio was now able to talk to animals! His new room changed into a magnificent rainforest, with animals and birds jumping around and flying about in celebration.

As the rest of the family celebrated with Antonio, Mirabel wanted to be alone. Although she was happy for her young cousin, Mirabel longed to have a shining moment of her own and wished she had a special gift to share.

As she wandered through the courtyard, a tile fell from the roof, crashing down next to her. She picked it up to check it but cut her hand on its sharp edge. Suddenly, cracks and splinters ripped through the House.

Mirabel rushed to her family, who were all still celebrating in Antonio's room.

"The House is in danger!" cried Mirabel.

Everyone stopped and stared at her. Wondering what Mirabel was worried about, Abuela asked her to show them the damage.

But there was nothing to see. No cracks. No splinters. Nothing.

Abuela glanced at Mirabel, a disappointed look in her eyes, before addressing the family. Her voice was full of confidence as she explained there was nothing wrong with La Casa Madrigal.

As Julieta prepared a remedy for Mirabel's hand, they talked about what had happened. Everyone thought Mirabel made the story up to ruin Antonio's night. But she insisted she would never do that.

"I wish you could see yourself the way I do," said Julieta. "You are perfect, just like this. You're just as special as anyone else in this family."

Julieta continued to try and cheer Mirabel up, but Mirabel insisted, "I know what I saw."

Julieta sighed. "Mira, my brother Bruno lost his way in this family... I don't want the same for you. Get some sleep. You'll feel better tomorrow."

But Mirabel couldn't sleep. Instead, she went out onto the tiled roof close to Abuela's window. She placed her hand on the wall - everything still seemed fine.

Then, Mirabel heard Abuela talking to a picture of Pedro. Abuela knew their home and magic were in danger. Just like her son Bruno - whose gift was the ability to see visions of the future - had predicted. Bruno had left the family years ago and no one knew where he'd gone to, although he still had a room in a tower at their home that had been left empty.

Mirabel was lost in thought as she listened to Abuela confess her worries to the picture of her husband.

Mirabel knew what she had to do: it was up to her to save the magic and the family.

She reassured their home, Casita, that she would do everything she possibly could, although she wasn't sure where to begin.

"I have no idea how to save a miracle," she admitted.

The next day, Mirabel learnt from Dolores, her older cousin with super hearing, that Luisa was up all night sweating - Luisa never sweated. Thinking this could be related to the problems with the magic, Mirabel decided to go and question her sister.

Mirabel found Luisa in town. She had a long list of jobs from the villagers she needed to complete. Luisa eventually admitted that she felt under a lot of pressure, and that she might have felt the cracks, too. Luisa told Mirabel she worried that if she lost her super strength, she would lose the only thing that made her feel useful to the villagers and a part of the family.

Mirabel was stunned into silence and simply wrapped her big sister in a hug. "I think you really need a break," she said.

Luisa squeezed back – very tightly – and breathed a huge sigh of relief. She looked at her sister and said, "You want to find a secret about the magic... go to Bruno's tower, find his last vision."

"Vision? Vision of what?" asked Mirabel.

"No one knows, they never found it," answered Luisa. When she hurried back to work, Mirabel reminded her to take a break.

"You're a good one, Sis," said Luisa. "Maybe I will."

Mirabel went back to the Casita, making sure to avoid Abuela. As she headed towards Bruno's tower, she noticed the candle. Its eternal flame was starting to flicker. Quickening her pace, Mirabel approached the set of stairs that led to Bruno's tower. His door was cobwebbed and lifeless. Stepping through, she found herself looking up at a winding stone stairway. Moments later, Antonio's toucan friend, Pico, landed next to her and smiled.

Mirabel began the long walk to the top. It took her all night, but as she reached the end, she noticed the final section of steps was no longer there.

"Don't suppose you could get me over there?" Mirabel asked Pico.

Pico hopped up and down on a nearby rope, which gave Mirabel an idea. Using the rope, Mirabel was able to secure it to a boulder sat on the other side, before swinging herself across.

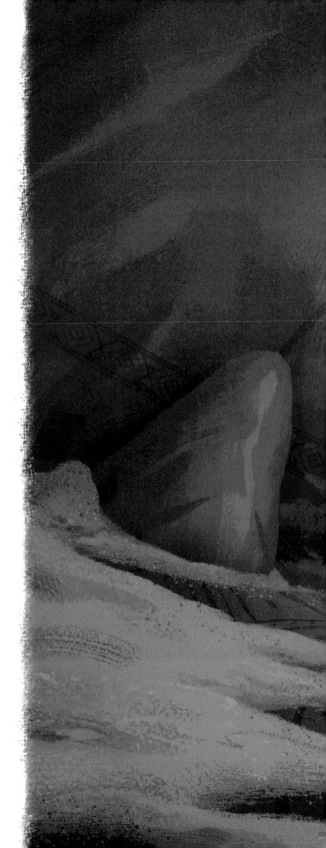

Safely on the other side, Mirabel continued her journey. She soon found herself in a room where a stream of sand fell from a hole in the ceiling.

Mirabel noticed several emerald pieces within the sand. As she picked them up and pieced them together, the room began to shake and cracks appeared all around! Mirabel only just managed to escape before the sand, which was pouring much faster now, could block her only way out.

On the way back to her room, Mirabel realised she had to hurry up and find the answers she needed. Luisa was starting to lose her gift – she was struggling to even open a jar!

Mirabel studied the emerald pieces again. Putting them together like a jigsaw, she was finally able to see Bruno's vision – the one Abuela was so worried about. It showed Casita with cracks all through it, and at the vision's centre was Mirabel.

Suddenly, Mirabel's father appeared. He was about to tell her it was time for the family's special dinner with the Guzmáns – the son was going to propose to Isabela – when he spotted the vision.

Mirabel explained what had happened.

Shocked by what his daughter had told him, Agustín quickly took the vision from Mirabel, and told her not to say anything.

However, across the way was Dolores. She'd heard everything the pair had been talking about.

At the special meal, Mariano Guzmán got down on one knee to propose to Isabela. However, the cracks appeared again and rippled around the room. One appeared under Isabela. Surprised, she lost control of her powers for a moment and accidentally smacked Mariano's face with some flowers, breaking his nose!

Amongst the Madrigals' panic and the chaos of the worried animals rushing around, the Guzmáns left. They were not impressed by what happened, and neither was Abuela. Despite Luisa losing her gift and Isabela's ruined proposal, Alma did her best to reassure everyone in the Encanto.

"We are fine! The magic is strong!" Alma called out to the scared villagers, who could see the damage all across the House.

At that moment, Mirabel saw rats carrying off the vision pieces!

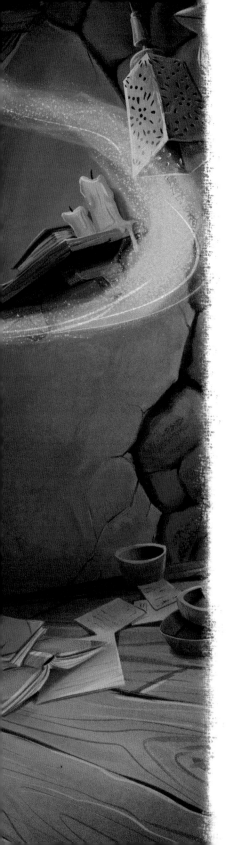

Mirabel slipped away and quietly followed the rats through a hidden entrance behind the walls and into a dark corridor.

Suddenly, a flash of lightning revealed her uncle, Bruno!

Their eyes met for a single moment before he raced off. Mirabel soon caught up with him.

Bruno now lived in a new room hidden in the House, away from everyone. He felt it was better for them all to think he had left, especially as he felt his visions weren't helping his family, only upsetting them.

Mirabel understood how he was feeling and how similar they were. She, too, felt like she had nothing to offer their family other than disappointment.

Bruno told Mirabel that the vision she saw, with her at the centre of everything, wasn't finished. He'd paused the vision and smashed it to pieces before finding out the end. He was worried it would confirm Abuela's fears about Mirabel's negative effect on the family's magic.

While he didn't know exactly how the vision would end, he did offer Mirabel a guess: "The fate of our entire family... it's gonna come down to you."

Moments later, Antonio and all his animal friends showed up. Pico and the others had told Antonio everything Mirabel had been up to with the shards and finding Bruno. Her young cousin was ready to help.

Mirabel decided now was the time to take the next step in her plan to save the family. She needed Bruno to have another vision.

Bruno said they needed a big space and Antonio offered his bedroom.

Mirabel encouraged Bruno, holding his hands, and he brought her into the vision. When it grew dark, Bruno wanted to end it, but Mirabel gave his hand a supportive squeeze and said, "The family needs you."

As magic glowed around him, a vision in emerald appeared. It showed Mirabel and Isabela hugging.

"Embrace her, and you will see the way," said Bruno.

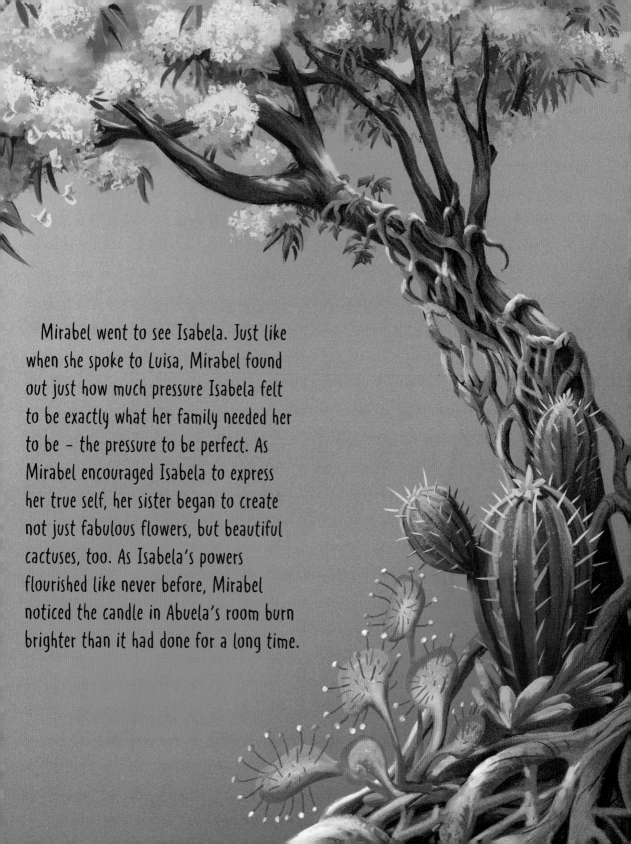

Mirabel went to see Isabela. Just like when she spoke to Luisa, Mirabel found out just how much pressure Isabela felt to be exactly what her family needed her to be – the pressure to be perfect. As Mirabel encouraged Isabela to express her true self, her sister began to create not just fabulous flowers, but beautiful cactuses, too. As Isabela's powers flourished like never before, Mirabel noticed the candle in Abuela's room burn brighter than it had done for a long time.

The plants and cactuses grew up and around the House. They were beautiful. Isabela had just begun to hug Mirabel when...

... "What have you done?" cried Abuela. She couldn't see that Mirabel had helped Isabela finally be herself. Abuela only saw her young granddaughter as the root of all the trouble the Madrigals were facing. "Our home is dying because of you!" she cried.

A tremor shook the entire Encanto. Mirabel told her grandmother the House was dying because no one in the family would ever be good enough for their abuela.

Suddenly, the house began to collapse all around them. Mirabel made a dash for the candle, but soon she stood in the centre of a pile of rubble as the house was no more. The candle was simply ash in Mirabel's hands.

Devastated by what she believed was all her fault, Mirabel ran away from the Encanto.

Mirabel made it as far as the river Abuela had crossed all those years ago with her husband, their three triplets and the villagers.

She looked at her reflection in the water, feeling lost and alone. A moment later, Abuela arrived.

Mirabel's grandmother explained the last time she'd been at this river was when her husband, Pedro, died – the day the Encanto was made.

Ever since that day, Abuela admitted she had been afraid, and that fear had led her to push her family harder and harder, not realising the damage she was causing. Abuela admitted she'd been the one to break the family, not Mirabel.

"I asked my Pedro for help," said Abuela. "Mirabel... he sent me you."

The pair embraced, understanding that together, they could put things right. Golden butterflies began to fly around them, just as Bruno arrived. To his surprise, Abuela hugged him, too!

The trio rode back to the Encanto.

"We're gonna be okay," Mirabel told the family. She explained how they aren't just defined by what they show on the outside, it's who they are on the inside that counts, too. Abuela agreed.

One by one, the Madrigals started to talk about their concerns and worries. As they became more confident in expressing how they truly felt, the magic began to glow bright again.

Soon, everyone began rebuilding Casita. Mirabel placed the final piece, the front doorknob, on the door.

WHOOSH!

The House came back to life in a fabulous flourish, sending an explosion of butterflies whizzing over the entire Encanto, mending the cracks and restoring the magic, including all the Madrigal family's gifts.

The family surrounded Mirabel in a loving embrace. Although they weren't the perfect family, the Madrigals cared for each other very much, and Mirabel finally knew she was where she truly belonged.